# The Last Night of the
L

K



ROUGH TRADE BOOKS

# *The Last Night of the Leamington Licker*

The last of a long Monday afternoon. The boy and his mother got up to leave, the boy chasing his straw around the bottom of the glass to suck up the final drop of Vimto, the mother adjusting her hat and buttoning her woollen coat right up to the top though it was still warm outside.

The boy held out a chewed pencil stub and a small maroon vinyl notepad with 'Autographs' printed in gold on the cover. "Can you sign my book?"

Randy found a blank page and signed his name.

"And can you write 'boxer'. So I can remember," said the boy.

Randy wrote 'Middleweight Boxing Champion of the World 1951' under his name, then crossed out the 1951, wrote the day's date—16.5.66—next to it and handed back the autograph book.

The boy looked at the page and put the book back into his satchel.

"Thanks Mr Turpin," said the woman and she lead the boy out of the cafe.

Randy cleared the table and wiped it down with a dish cloth. When the place was busy it was easy to shut things out but after lunch, when it was quiet, he'd find himself leaning on the counter and remembering things he'd rather forget. His first wife Mary had turned up with that American witch Adele Daniels and they'd sat by the window cursing him. He'd ignored them as best he could and eventually they'd vanished. The only remaining customer was a man in a cheap blue suit who'd flipped his tie over his shoulder when his food had arrived as if he had work to do and was now smothering the remains of his egg and chips in more brown sauce.

For the previous half hour the man had been bending his ear about Cooper versus Ali and how Cooper was gonna win this time and Randy had shaken his head and told him Cooper was a bleeder, and he was losing his hair, which told you something, and it would all be over in six rounds and if he didn't know that then he didn't know nothing. He'd offered the man 10-1 that that's exactly what was going to happen and he'd shaken on it but the man had only wanted to bet a lousy shilling.

Randy hovered over him with the dishcloth in his hand hoping it would encourage him to finish his plate and leave so he could start closing up but the man just wanted to go on talking about Henry Cooper some more. Randy was halfway through telling him again exactly why Ali was too quick for Cooper but the man seemed to think he was only saying that because Ali was one of 'his lot' and that 'the coloureds' always stuck up for each other.

Randy recalled somebody telling him right back at the beginning of it all that there was a saying in boxing that went 'two blacks don't make a fight.' You had to remember that. The white guy is the nice guy and that's just the way it is.

There was nothing else he could think of to say about Cooper that the man might want to hear so Randy went back behind the counter to tidy up. He was crating up the empty milk bottles when the bell above the cafe door jangled.

A man entered, sleeves rolled up, sweat stains under his arms, old blue army tattoos on weathered skin, sucking hard on a cigarette. He walked straight up to the counter, "Mosh said you was looking for me. So I got something for you."

The man took a crumpled bank note from his pocket and slapped it on the counter-top. Randy stared at it.

"It was ten pounds I loaned you Ronnie, not ten bob."

"It's a start innit?" Ronnie winked, "Anyway, can't stop. See you later Sooty. Tell Mosh I bin in else he'll keep on at me."

Ronnie grinned and ambled out the door. A half smile played out on Randy's face but not on the weary bones beneath his skin. For the thousandth time at least he re-read the sign that he'd hung on the wall behind the counter. It was like the punchline to a bad joke: THAT WHICH SELDOM COMES BACK TO HIM WHO WAITS IS THE MONEY HE LENDS TO HIS FRIENDS. Not that Ronnie had been any kind of friend. Not somebody he'd helped out because their car needed fixing or because they were behind with their rent or because they had an idea for a business that the banks wouldn't touch or because they needed 'just a few pounds—just for a couple of days.' Ronnie was a bloke he hardly knew who happened to catch Randy in a pub, half-cut and out to impress some birds with a demonstration of his generosity.

He folded up the bank note and put it in his pocket.

"You still got some fans then Randy," said the man in the blue suit who had finally finished the last of his food and was lighting up a Player's, "you're still getting asked for your autograph. Maybe you could make a go of this place yet." The man waved his cigarette around the room like he was giving it some kind of priestly blessing but Randy saw the smirk on his greasy lips and guessed that, though he might not know anything about boxing, the one thing he did know like everybody else in town knew was that the cafe was condemned. Compulsory purchase order. All set to be demolished and turned into a council car park and had been even before Randy had been sweet-talked into buying it. He had the feeling these days that the whole town was joining in to laugh up their sleeves at the state of the Licker. He could hear the mutterings and the whispers whistling around his head the way the wind used to whip across the clifftops on those long walks in North Wales.

And anyway it had only been the conversation about Henry Cooper that had pricked the sullen schoolboy's attention and got him bringing out his book. He hadn't come looking for him. Mostly, the only ones that did just brought bad news or trouble. Like Ronnie with his mickey-taking five bob or the man the previous week who'd cycled all the way from Coventry just so he could start something and try and land a punch on him. And Randy would've just smashed him right there on the linoleum if Mosh hadn't have been standing by to talk him out of it and let him settle for just stomping buckles in his bicycle wheels. They'd watched the man wobble off down Russell Street like a circus clown. That had been a laugh at least.

When the man in the blue suit finally left Randy flipped the closed sign and locked the door. He cleared away the tables, dumped the crockery into the sink, pulled on a pair of yellow rubber gloves and set the water running. After washing up and stacking the dishes he counted the day's takings in the till. It didn't take long. He looked at the coins and the handful of notes and remembered a time when he'd have spent double that amount on a pair of silk socks.

He put the money in a small safe under the counter and then telephoned Mosh and told him about Ronnie's visit. Mosh his old schoolfriend and his blood brother. Mosh who always said that he might not have even been there if he hadn't ducked that time Randy had been throwing a bayonet at an apple on his head when they'd been kids. Mosh saying 'you could've killed me, you could've killed me' and Randy thinking that it was one big joke and pulling out the knife from the backyard door and getting him to stand up against it again. And when he had, even though he was shaking, Randy knowing for sure that he'd do anything for him. Then they'd sliced their palms with the bayonet and gripped hands like the cowboys and indians they'd seen in the Saturday morning pictures until the blood ran down to their wrists.

He asked Mosh if he'd heard from anybody else that they'd been chasing around town for money but Mosh had nothing good to say to him and he sounded just as sad as anything when he was saying it.

"They got me now," said Randy, "I'm done for."

"What are you talking about?" said Mosh and Randy could hear him on the other end of the line lighting up a cigarette and breathing in and breathing out slowly the way he always did when he was pretending he wasn't worried about something.

"I got a letter Saturday. Final notice. We've run out of time."

"We could go back to that fellow in Birmingham," said Mosh, "he said he'd pay up."

"You know he never will."

"What about you go back and see Mr S? Give it another shot. I'll come with you this time."

Randy sighed. From the flat above the cafe he heard Gwen and one of the children squabbling and then a door slamming and then silence.

"You listening Randy?" said Mosh, "I said why don't we go and see Jack?"

"No point. I told you what happened last time." said Randy although he hadn't told him what had really happened at all. He had never told anybody.

He'd gone to London and visited Jack Solomons' gym in Soho. There'd been the usual crowd of fighters on their way up or on their way down or somewhere in between. It didn't matter where they were because Jolly Jack could always find a way to turn a buck off of any of them. And then there were the gamblers and the gangsters and the spivs. One time they'd have seen him enter and the whole place would've froze and he'd have been shaking hand after hand and the hard men would've been slapping his back and the newspapermen with their trilbies and shorthand notepads would've been hustling for a quote. This time it was like he was invisible. He'd even had to check himself in the mirror on the wall of the gym to make sure he was really there at all.

He'd made it as far as Solomons' office without anybody asking what he was doing and he'd entered without knocking. Solomons sat at his desk and barely acknowledged him. Then, as polite as anything, he'd asked him if there was any way possible that he could get hold of the money he was sure Mr Solomons remembered he'd lodged with him. Solomons had shown more interest in the fat cigar he was rolling between his fingers and the gold cigar cutter he had in his other hand that at first Randy had taken to be a knuckleduster.

"What money's that?" Solomons had said as he'd cut the end from the cigar and lit it up.

"The £20,000 I asked you to look after for me. The money for the film rights to the second Sugar Ray fight."

"There is no money, Randolph."

Randy had leaned across the desk and yelled at him that there fucking well was and he knew it but Solomons just waved his hand and the next thing Randy knew he was being dragged out through the gym and back out the door on to the street and this time everybody had stopped what they were doing to watch.

He'd had a few in a pub called the Red Lion and then decided to go back to Solomons to try again. This time he hadn't made it in the front door. Two big men had grabbed him from behind and marched him down an alleyway and slammed his head against a damp brick wall and hissed in his ear that he better quit asking around after money cos its gone and it ain't coming back and if he doesn't learn that then the next time he won't even get the chance to run away home. And then, as calm as he could be, he'd turned around and looked at them and saw that these big men were nothing much and he could've dropped them both as easy as knocking the skin of boiled milk but he knew they were just the top of it and there were plenty more ready to take their place and he'd never beat them all and that's the way it was and that's the way it would always be. He'd let the men hit him a few times and he'd covered up and he'd rolled the punches as well as he could with four fists flying at him. After they'd gone he went back to the pub until it closed and then walked in the rain to the railway station. He'd sat on a bench in the cold, his head throbbing and an egg-sized lump slowly blooming over his eye where his head had hit the wall, waiting all night for the first train back to Leamington.

"This is it Mosh," said Randy, "they're screwing the lid on my coffin and they ain't even waiting 'til I'm dead." He hung the phone back on the cradle, walked out into the yard and fetched a metal bucket. He came back into the cafe, stacked the chairs on the tables and set about mopping the floor.

That morning he'd got home from Soho, the story he'd told Gwen was that he'd been wrestling and the crowd had got out of hand. She hadn't known anything about him going to see Solomons in any case and she didn't ask any more about it. She'd cleaned the graze on his cheek and put the steak they were going to eat for dinner on his swollen forehead. Then Randy had fried it up for breakfast and they'd shared it and even though she'd said she couldn't believe she was eating it after seeing where it had been she'd had to admit that he knew how to fry steak just right.

After that he'd had to go and lay down because his head was spinning and when he'd finally managed to fall asleep after silently screaming murder on Solomons and his gangster friends who'd robbed him blind he'd had the first of the terrible dreams.

Larry Gains was there at the end of the bed and his six foot plus frame was swaying left and right like he was working the heavy bag and he was sneering "You should have come to see me Randy. That night I sent for you at the Seven Stars."

"I'd already signed with George," Randy heard himself saying though he knew his lips weren't moving.

"And you went with George and you went with Jack. Jolly Jack Solomons, born with six fingers so he could rob you better. Bought and sold. Yes master! You hadn't been so damn good they'd have fixed it so you'd turn up and lose to every blue-eyed boy old man Solomons could muster... I'd have looked after you. I'd have made you a champion."

"I was a champion. I am a champion. They can't take that away."

"You fell in with the wrong crowd."

"I was already in with the wrong crowd. I was trying to find a way out."

"You're easily lead."

"Yeah, up the bloody garden path. I just wanted people to like me."

"They all loved your money. You tried asking for any of it back?"

And Gains was laughing, a big booming laugh that shook the bedroom windows like a train was going by and then the voices of George and Jack and Sugar Ray and Bobo Olson and a hundred other people crowding around him and he's flat on his back on the canvas and the lights are shining down on him and he can't move at all let alone get up and he's screaming and the referee is counting but every number is ten. Every number is ten. Every number is ten.

Gwen had woken him up all soaked with sweat with the sheets gripped in his fist like wraps and she'd said what's the matter you look like you've seen a ghost and he'd told her don't worry I had a bad dream but he didn't tell her that Gains was still there in the room leaning against the wardrobe laughing at him. And even when he'd screwed up his eyes to blank him out he'd heard all the others whispering in his ears and they were daring him to open his eyes to see if they were really there. And when he had opened them they were all around him and they'd never ever left.

He worked the mop, taking pride in the way the arcs of soapy water made the floor shine and then he took out a cloth and buffed the linoleum so that when he kneeled down right up close he could see a blurred face looking back at him. While he was staring at it, trying to work out if he even recognized himself any more, the voices came and they were mocking him about all the things that had been, that could have been, that should've been. He muttered curses under his breath willing them to shut up until he heard a knock on the door and he leapt to his feet in case the man peering in through the glass had thought that he was praying.

"How you doing champ?" said a fat man who had somehow squeezed himself into a three piece suit.

"I'd almost given up on you John," Randy said and he shook the man's hand and let him inside.

"Took a little while longer than I thought. Had to run around all over, but I got something in the end." The man jerked the handle of the leather sports bag he was carrying.

Randy locked the door behind them and ushered the man over to a table in the far corner of the cafe underneath a poster advertising Warwick Castle. He unstacked the chairs and then fetched two bottles of beer from the fridge. John had settled in his seat and was looking around the place. The last time Randy had seen him had been on a wrestling bill at a rundown theatre in Dudley and he'd entered the ring wearing a threadbare ermine cape and been announced as Lord John Silver. He looked worse in a suit. He looked as uncomfortable as if he'd dressed for a court appearance or a job interview.

John sucked on the beer and lit an Embassy. "I don't want to upset you Licker but this place can't be making you much. No wonder you're in trouble for money. You want to come back on the wrestling."

Randy said he'd think about it but he knew that he wouldn't. He'd done the circuit for longer than he should have which is to say he never should have had to do it at all. Twenty pounds a night for the shame of parading around with men pretending to be masked executioners or crocodile wrestling champions from the Congo or landed gentry with council house accents. And when the halls had emptied and the ring was taken down and the vans were all packed they'd sit at a lock-in somewhere and drink until the money ran out so the next day they had to start all over again. Was that any way for a champion to live? Behind Lord John's shoulder a vision of Sugar Ray Robinson was shaking his head.

They sat in silence drinking their beer. John could see Randy was staring down at the sports bag on the floor so he unzipped it and took out a package wrapped in brown paper and put it on the table, "My man said you don't have to give it straight back. Not until you're ready."

"Tell him he'll be able to come and get it whenever he wants," said Randy.

"How's your Mrs?" said John. He jerked a thumb towards the ceiling.

"Sick of the sight of me." Randy smiled.

"And you're sure you don't want to come back out on the road with us?" John laughed and then started coughing and wiped his mouth with the back of the sleeve of his suit jacket so a slick of spit ran parallel with the chalk stripes.

"You wanna pack them in."

Randy pointed at the packet of Embassy on the table and John saw that as an invitation to take out another and spark it up. He rolled the empty beer bottle between his palms, chinking his rings against the glass in the hope that somehow that might summon another bottle but Randy just sat there staring at the package not saying anything.

"Alright then champ," said John after a few minutes, "I'll leave you be. Got a hundred miles to drive back in any case."

He hoisted himself out of his seat and Randy shook his hand and showed him out.

Randy locked the package in the safe and let himself out into the backyard. In the corner of the yard was a small shed with a corrugated iron roof. He went inside and sat on an old army blanket on a camp bed he'd set up for the nights when Gwen had kicked him out of the flat upstairs. He listened to the music coming from an open window on the first floor. Anne Shelton was singing *Body And Soul.* It was a record he'd bought for Gwen a long time ago and she'd played it over and over until it hissed and crackled and clicked. She'd told him she'd played it every night he was away from home fighting when she'd stay up and pray he'd be coming home safely. And she played it these days to remind her of how things used to be and Randy knew if she was playing it now, with the window wide open, it was a signal that she'd forgiven him again and wanted him to come back upstairs.

He listened until the song reached the last verse. Shelton was singing about storms and cold grey winters. When she sang the line about magic he pushed the shed door closed with his boot and lay on the bed. The record ended and he heard it start up again. He lay there and listened as it played over and over. He closed his eyes.

He was flat on his back in the ring. There was the taste of blood in his mouth. Like the rumble of a distant ocean he could hear the crowd roaring his name. Then growing louder he could make out that the crowd were jeering and above him the referee's shirt cuff was zig-zagging over his face and he heard him counting and every number was ten.

When he woke it was dark and for a second he couldn't remember where he was or if he was even alive. He knew what he had to do. It was the only way he would ever be able to escape from the shadow of who he used to be.

Randy stepped into the yard. The upstairs windows were closed. The sky was clear and dark. The waning moon cast no light. He quietly let himself back into the cafe. He took some paper and a pen from a shelf under the counter and then took the package from the safe. In a seat by the window in the yellow wash of a street lamp he started writing. 'Naturally, they will say my mind was disturbed, but it is not...' He stopped writing and put down the pen. He stared at the package and peeled away the brown paper wrapping. The gun was cold and heavy in his hand. It was loaded, as he had been promised it would be. In the morning he'd say goodbye to the children.

# Afterword

Randolph Adolphus Turpin (known as The Leamington Licker) was born in Leamington Spa on June 7 1928 and committed suicide on May 17 1966. In 1951, as a huge underdog, he beat Sugar Ray Robinson to become the Middleweight Champion of the World. He had been champion for only 64 days when he was defeated in a rematch. Turpin was never able to regain the title and when his boxing career was over he gradually faded into poverty and bitter obscurity. Reckless with his earnings and poorly managed and advised he had loaned out cash that was never repaid and was hounded by the taxman for money which he claimed he had never seen. He ended up broke, running a failing transport cafe in the back streets of Leamington Spa. He was inducted into the International Boxing Hall of Fame in 2001.

There have been numerous biographical accounts of Turpin's life that have charted his fight career and tried to present the facts that lead to his death. The best of these remains the documentary *64 Day Hero* (dir. Franco Rosso, 1985). The preceding story is not an attempt to add to these. It is a creative work aimed at Camus' idea of fiction being the lie through which we tell the truth. Turpin's story was first told to me by my grandfather who had known him in his early years. I dedicate this to the memory of Charlie Forde and to Randolph Turpin.